The
Thesmophoriazusae

Aristophanes

Copyright Notice

CONTENTS

Dramatis Personae

EURIPIDES

MNESILOCHUS, Father-in-law of Euripides

AGATHON

SERVANT OF AGATHON

HERALD

WOMEN

CLISTHENES

A MAGISTRATE

A SCYTHIAN POLICEMAN

Scene

Behind the orchestra are two buildings, one the house of the poet AGATHON, the other the Thesmophorion. EURIPIDES enters from the right, at a rapid pace, with an air of searching for something; his father-in-law MNESILOCHUS, who is extremely aged, follows him as best he can, with an obviously painful expenditure of effort.

MNESILOCHUS: Great Zeus! will the swallow never appear to end the winter of my discontent? Why the fellow has kept me on the run ever since early this morning; he wants to kill me, that's certain. Before I lose my spleen antirely, Euripides, can you at least tell me where you are leading me?

EURIPIDES: What need for you to hear what you are going to see?

MNESILOCHUS: How is that? Repeat it. No need for me to hear....

EURIPIDES: What you are going to see.

MNESILOCHUS: Nor consequently to see....

EURIPIDES: What you have to hear.

MNESILOCHUS: What is this wiseacre stuff you are telling me? I must neither see nor hear?

EURIPIDES: Ah! but you have two things there that are essentially distinct.

MNESILOCHUS: Seeing and hearing?

EURIPIDES: Undoubtedly.

MNESILOCHUS: In what way distinct?

EURIPIDES: In this way. Formerly, when Aether separated the elements and bore the animals that were moving in her bosom, she wished to endow them with sight, and so made the eye round like the sun's disc and bored ears in the form of a funnel.

MNESILOCHUS: And because of this funnel I neither see nor hear. Ah! great gods! I am delighted to know it. What a fine thing it is to talk with wise men!

EURIPIDES: I will teach you many another thing of the sort.

MNESILOCHUS: That's well to know; but first of all I should like to find out how to grow lame, so that I need not have to follow you all about.

EURIPIDES: Come, hear and give heed!

MNESILOCHUS: I'm here and waiting.

EURIPIDES Do you see that little door?

MNESILOCHUS: Yes, certainly.

EURIPIDES: Silence!

MNESILOCHUS: Silence about what? About the door?

EURIPIDES: Pay attention!

MNESILOCHUS: Pay attention and be silent about the door? Very well.

EURIPIDES: That is where Agathon, the celebrated tragic poet, dwells.

MNESILOCHUS: Who is this Agathon?

EURIPIDES: He's a certain Agathon....

MNESILOCHUS: Swarthy, robust of build?

EURIPIDES: No, another.

MNESILOCHUS: I have never seen him. He has a big beard?

EURIPIDES: Have you never seen him?

MNESILOCHUS: Never, so far as I know.

EURIPIDES: And yet you have made love to him. Well, it must have been without knowing who he was. [The door of AGATHON'S house opens.] Ah! let us step aside; here is one of his slaves bringing a brazier and some myrtle branches; no doubt he is going to offer a sacrifice and pray for a happy poetical inspiration for Agathon.

SERVANT OF AGATHON: [standing on the threshold; solemnly] Silence! oh, people! keep your mouths sedately shut! The chorus of the Muses is moulding songs at my master's hearth. Let the winds hold their breath in the silent Aether! Let the azure waves cease murmuring on the shore!....

MNESILOCHUS: Bombax.

EURIPIDES: Be still! I want to hear what he is saying.

SERVANT: ....Take your rest, ye winged races, and you, ye savage inhabitants of the woods, cease from your erratic wandering....

MNESILOCHUS: [more loudly] Bom-balobombax.

SERVANT: ....for Agathon, our master, the sweet-voiced poet, is going....

MNESILOCHUS: ....to be made love to?

SERVANT: Whose voice is that?

MNESILOCHUS: It's the silent Aether.

SERVANT: ....is going to construct the framework of a drama. He is rounding fresh poetical forms, he is polishing them in the lathe and is welding them; he is hammering out sentences and metaphors; he is working up his subect like soft wax. First he models it and then he casts it in bronze....

MNESILOCHUS: ....and sways his buttocks amorously.

SERVANT: Who is the rustic that approaches this sacred enclosure?

MNESILOCHUS: Take care of yourself and of your sweet-voiced poet! I have a strong tool here both well rounded and well polished, which will pierce your enclosure and penetrate you.

SERVANT: Old man, you must have been a very insolent fellow in your youth!

EURIPIDES: [to the SERVANT] Let him be, friend, and, quick, go and call Agathon to me.

SERVANT: It's not worth the trouble, for he will soon be here himself. He has started to compose, and in winter it is never possible to round off strophes without coming to the sun to excite the imagination.

EURIPIDES: And what am I to do?

SERVANT: Wait till he gets here. [He goes into the house.]

EURIPIDES: Oh, Zeus! what hast thou in store for me to-day?

MNESILOCHUS: Great gods, what is the matter now? What are you grumbling and groaning for? Tell me; you must not conceal anything from your father-in-law.

EURIPIDES: Some great misfortune is brewing against me.

MNESILOCHUS: What is it?

EURIPIDES: This day will decide whether it is all over with Euripides or not.

MNESILOCHUS: But how? Neither the tribunals nor the Senate are sitting, for it is the third day of the Thesmophoria.

EURIPIDES: That is precisely what makes me tremble; the women have plotted my ruin, and to-day they are to gather in the

Temple of Demeter to execute their decision.

MNESILOCHUS: What have they against you?

EURIPIDES: Because I mishandle them in my tragedies.

MNESILOCHUS: By Posidon, you would seem to have thoroughly deserved your fate. But how are you going to get out of the mess?

EURIPIDES: I am going to beg Agathon, the tragic poet, to go to the Thesmophoria.

MNESILOCHUS: And what is he to do there?

EURIPIDES: He would mingle with the women, and stand up for me, if needful.

MNESILOCHUS: Would be present or secretly?

EURIPIDES: Secretly, dressed in woman's clothes.

MNESILOCHUS: That's a clever notion, thoroughly worthy of you. The prize for trickery is ours. [The door of AGATHON'S house opens.]

EURIPIDES: Silence!

MNESILOCHUS: What's the matter?

EURIPIDES: Here comes Agathon.

MNESILOCHUS: Where, where?

EURIPIDES: That's the man they are bringing out yonder on the eccyclema. [AGATHON appears on the eccyclema, softly reposing on a bed, clothed in a saffron tunic, and surrounded with feminine toilet articles.]

MNESILOCHUS: I am blind then! I see no man here, I only see Cyrene.

EURIPIDES: Be still! He is getting ready to sing.

MNESILOCHUS: What subtle trill, I wonder, is he going to warble to us?

AGATHON: [He now sings a selection from one of his tragedies, taking first the part of the leader of the chorus and then that of the whole chorus. As LEADER OF THE CHORUS] Damsels, with the sacred torch in hand, unite your dance to shouts of joy in honour of the nether goddesses; celebrate the freedom of your country. [As CHORUS] To what divinity is your homage addressed? I wish to mingle mine with it. [As LEADER OF THE CHORUS] Oh! Muse! glorify Phoebus with his golden bow, who erected the walls of the city of the Simois. [As CHORUS] To thee, oh Phoebus, I dedicate my most beauteous songs; to thee, the sacred victor in the poetical contests. [As LEADER OF THE CHORUS] And praise Artemis too, the maiden huntress, who wanders on the mountains and through the woods.... [As CHORUS] I, in my turn, celebrate the everlasting happiness of the chaste Artemis, the mighty daughter of Leto! [As LEADER OF THE CHORUS] ....and Leto and the tones of the Asiatic lyre, which wed so well with the dances of the Phrygian Graces. [As CHORUS] I do honour to the divine Leto and to the lyre, the mother of songs of male and noble strains. The eyes of the goddess sparkle while listening to our enthusiastic chants. Honour to the powerful Phoebus! Hail! thou blessed son of Leto.

MNESILOCHUS: Oh! ye venerable Genetyllides, what tender and voluptuous songs! They surpass the most lascivious kisses in sweetness; I feel a thrill of delight pass up me as I listen to them. [To EURIPIDES] Young man, if you are one, answer my questions, which I am borrowing from Aeschylus' "Lycurgeia." Whence comes this androgyne? What is his country? his dress? What contradictions his life shows! A lyre and a hair-net! A wrestling school oil flask and a girdle! What could be more contradictory? What relation has a mirror to a sword? [To AGATHON] And you yourself, who are you? Do you pretend to be a man? Where is your tool, pray? Where is the cloak, the footgear that belong to that sex? Are you a woman? Then where are your breasts? Answer me.

But you keep silent. Oh! just as you choose; your songs display your character quite sufficiently.

AGATHON: Old man, old man, I hear the shafts of jealousy whistling by my ears, but they do not hit me. My dress is in harmony with my thoughts. A poet must adopt the nature of his characters. Thus, if he is placing women on the stage, he must contract all their habits in his own person.

MNESILOCHUS: [aside] Then you make love horse-fashion when you are composing a Phaedra.

AGATHON: If the heroes are men, everything in him will be manly. What we don't possess by nature, we must acquire by imitation.

MNESILOCHUS: [aside] When you are staging Satyrs, call me; I will do my best to help you from behind, if I can get my tool up.

AGATHON: Besides, it is bad taste for a poet to be coarse and hairy. Look at the famous Ibycus, at Anacreon of Teos, and at Alcaeus, who handled music so well; they wore head-bands and found pleasure in the lascivious dances of Ionia. And have you not heard what a dandy Phrynichus was and how careful in his dress? For this reason his pieces were also beautiful, for the works of a poet are copied from himself.

MNESILOCHUS: Ah! so it is for this reason that Philocles, who is so hideous, writes hideous pieces; Xeno-cles, who is malicious, malicious ones, and Theognis, who is cold, such cold ones?

AGATHON: Yes, necessarily and unavoidably; and it is because I knew this that I have so well cared for my person.

MNESILOCHUS: How, in the gods' name?

EURIPIDES: Come, leave off badgering him; I was just the same at his age, when I began to write.

MNESILOCHUS: Ah! then, by Zeus! I don't envy you your fine manners.

EURIPIDES: [to AGATHON] But listen to the cause that brings me here.

AGATHON: Say on.

EURIPIDES: Agathon, wise is he who can compress many thoughts into few words. Struck by a most cruel misfortune, I come to you as a suppliant.

AGATHON: What are you asking?

EURIPIDES: The women purpose killing me to-day during the Thesmophoria, because I have dared to speak ill of them.

AGATHON: And what can I do for you in the matter?

EURIPIDES: Everything. Mingle secretly with the women by making yourself pass as one of themselves; then do you plead my cause with your own lips, and I am saved. You, and you alone, are capable of speaking of me worthily.

AGATHON: But why not go and defend yourself?

EURIPIDES Impossible. First of all, I am known; further, I have white hair and a long beard; whereas you, you are good-looking, charming, and are close-shaven; you are fair, delicate, and have a woman's voice.

AGATHON: Euripides!

EURIPIDES: Well?

AGATHON: Have you not said in one of your pieces, "You love to see the light, and don't you believe your father loves it too?"

EURIPIDES: Yes.

AGATHON: Then never you think I am going to expose myself in your stead; it would be madness. It's up to you to submit to the fate that overtakes you; one must not try to trick misfortune, but resign oneself to it with good grace.

MNESILOCHUS: You fairy! That's why your arse is so accessible to lovers.

EURIPIDES: But what prevents your going there?

AGATHON: I should run more risk than you would.

EURIPIDES: Why?

AGATHON: Why? I should look as if I were wanting to trespass on secret nightly pleasures of the women and to rape their Aphrodite.

MNESILOCHUS: [aside] Wanting to rape indeed! you mean wanting to be raped. Ah! great gods! a fine excuse truly!

EURIPIDES: Well then, do you agree?

AGATHON: Don't count upon it.

EURIPIDES: Oh! I am unfortunate indeed! I am undone!

MNESILOCHUS: Euripides, my friend, my son-in-law, never despair.

EURIPIDES: What can be done?

MNESILOCHUS: Send him to the devil and do with me as you like.

EURIPIDES: Very well then, since you devote yourself to my safety, take off your cloak first.

MNESILOCHUS: There, it lies on the ground. But what do you want to do with me?

EURIPIDES To shave off this beard of yours, and to remove all your other hair as well.

MNESILOCHUS: Do what you think fit; I yield myself entirely to you.

EURIPIDES: Agathon, you always have razors about you; lend me one.

AGATHON: Take it yourself, there, out of that case.

EURIPIDES: Thanks. [To MNESILOCHUS:] Now sit down and puff out your right cheek.

MNESILOCHUS: [as he is being shaved] Ow! Ow! Ow!

EURIPIDES What are you houting for? I'll cram a spit down your gullet, if you're not quiet.

MNESILOCHUS: Ow! Ow! Ow! Ow! Ow! [He jumps up and starts running away.]

EURIPIDES: Where are you running to now?

MNESILOCHUS: To the temple of the Eumenides. No, by Demeter! I won't let myself be gashed like that.

EURIPIDES: But you will get laughed at, with your face half-shaven like that.

MNESILOCHUS: Little care I.

EURIPIDES: In the gods' names, don't leave me in the lurch. Come here.

MNESILOCHUS: Oh! by the gods! [He turns reluctantly and resumes his seat.]

EURIPIDES Keep still and hold up your head. Why do you want to fidget about like this?

MNESILOCHUS: Mm, mm.

EURIPIDES: Well! why mm, mm? There! it's done and well done too!

MNESILOCHUS: Alas, I shall fight without armour.

EURIPIDES: Don't worry; you look charming. Do you want to see yourself?

MNESILOCHUS: Yes, I do; hand the mirror here.

EURIPIDES: Do you see yourself?

MNESILOCHUS: But this is not I, it is Clisthenes!

EURIPIDES: Stand up; I am now going to remove your hair. Bend down.

MNESILOCHUS: Alas! alas! they are going to grill me like a pig.

EURIPIDES: Come now, a torch or a lamp! Bend down and watch out for the tender end of your tool!

MNESILOCHUS: Aye, aye! but I'm afire! oh! oh! Water, water, neighbour, or my perineum will be alight!

EURIPIDES: Keep up your courage!

MNESILOCHUS: Keep my courage, when I'm being burnt up?

EURIPIDES: Come, cease your whining, the worst is over.

MNESILOCHUS: Oh! it's quite black, all burnt down there!

EURIPIDES Don't worry! Satyrus will wash it.

MNESILOCHUS: Woe to him who dares to wash me!

EURIPIDES: Agathon, you refuse to devote yourself to helping me; but at any rate lend me a tunic and a belt. You cannot say you have not got them.

AGATHON: Take them and use them as you like; I consent.

MNESILOCHUS: What shall I take?

EURIPIDES: First put on this long saffron-coloured robe.

MNESILOCHUS: By Aphrodite! what a sweet odour! how it smells of young male tools Hand it to me quickly. And the belt?

EURIPIDES: Here it is.

MNESILOCHUS: Now some rings for my legs.

EURIPIDES: You still want a hair-net and a head-dress.

AGATHON: Here is my night cap.

EURIPIDES: Ah! that's fine.

MNESILOCHUS: Does it suit me?

AGATHON: It could not be better.

EURIPIDES: And a short mantle?

AGATHON: There's one on the couch; take it.

EURIPIDES: He needs slippers.

AGATHON: Here are mine.

MNESILOCHUS: Will they fit me? [To AGATHON] You don't like a loose fit.

AGATHON: Try them on. Now that you have all you need, let me be taken inside. [The eccyclema turns and AGATHON disappears.]

EURIPIDES: You look for all the world like a woman. But when you talk, take good care to give your voice a woman's tone.

MNESILOCHUS: [falsetto] I'll try my best.

EURIPIDES: Come, get yourself to the temple.

MNESILOCHUS: No, by Apollo, not unless you swear to me....

EURIPIDES: What?

MNESILOCHUS: ....that, if anything untoward happen to me, you will leave nothing undone to save me.

EURIPIDES: Very well! I swear it by the Aether, the dwelling-place of the king of the gods.

MNESILOCHUS: Why not rather swear it by the sons of Hippocrates?

EURIPIDES: Come, I swear it by all the gods, both great and small.

MNESILOCHUS: Remember, it's the heart, and not the tongue, that has sworn; for the oaths of the tongue concern me but little.

EURIPIDES: Hurry up! The signal for the meeting has just been raised on the Temple of Demeter. Farewell. [They both depart. The scene changes to the interior of the Thesmophorion, where the women who form the chorus are assembled. MNESILOCHUS: enters, in his feminine attire, striving to act as womanly as possible, and giving his voice as female a pitch and lilt as he can; he pretends to be addressing his slave-girl.]

MNESILOCHUS: Here, Thratta, follow me. Look, Thratta, at the cloud of smoke that arises from all these lighted torches. Ah! beautiful Thesmophorae! grant me your favours, protect me, both within the temple and on my way back! Come, Thratta, put down the basket and take out the cake, which I wish to offer to the two goddesses. Mighty divinity, oh, Demeter, and thou, Persephone, grant that I may be able to offer you many sacrifices; above all things, grant that I may not be recognized. Would that my well-holed daughter might marry a man as rich as he is foolish and silly, so that she may have nothing to do but amuse herself. But where can a place be found for hearing well? Be off, Thratta, be off; slaves have no right to be present at this gathering. [He sits down amongst the women.]

WOMAN HERALD: Silence! Silence! Pray to the Thesmophorae, Demeter and Cora; pray to Plutus, Calligenia, Curotrophus, the Earth, Hermes and the Graces, that all may happen for the best at this gathering, both for the greatest advantage of Athens and for our own personal happiness! May the award be given her who, by both deeds and words, has most deserved it from the Athenian people and from the women! Address these prayers to heaven and demand happiness for yourselves. Io Paean! Io Paean! Let us rejoice!

CHORUS: [singing] May the gods deign to accept our vows and our prayers! Oh! almighty Zeus, and thou, god with the golden lyre, who reignest on sacred Delos, and thou, oh, invincible virgin, Pallas, with the eyes of azure and the spear of gold, who protectest our illustrious city, and thou, the daughter of the beautiful Leto, queen of the forests, who art adored under many names, hasten hither at my call. Come, thou mighty Posidon, king of the Ocean, leave thy stormy whirlpools of Nereus; come, goddesses of the seas, come, ye nymphs, who wander on the mountains. Let us unite our voices to the sounds of the golden lyre, and may wisdom preside at the gathering of the noble matrons of Athens.

WOMAN HERALD: Address your prayers to the gods and goddesses of Olympus, of Delphi, Delos and all other places; if there be a man who is plotting against the womenfolk or who, to injure them, is proposing peace to Euripides and the Medes, or who aspires to usurping the tyranny, plots the return of a tyrant, or unmasks a supposititious child; or if there be a slave who, a confidential party to a wife's intrigues, reveals them secretly to her husband, or who, entrusted with a message, does not deliver the same faithfully; if there be a lover who fulfils naught of what he has promised a woman, whom he has abused on the strength of his lies; if there be an old woman who seduces the lover of a maiden by dint of her presents and treacherously receives him in her house; if there be a host or hostess who sells false measure, pray the gods that they will overwhelm them with their wrath, both them and their families, and that they may reserve all their favours for you.

CHORUS: [singing] Let us ask the fulfilment of these wishes both for the city and for the people, and may the wisest of us cause her opinion to be accepted. But woe to those women who break their oaths, who speculate on the public misfortune, who seek to alter the laws and the decrees, who reveal our secrets to the foe and admit the Medes into our territory so that they may devastate it! I declare them both impious and criminal. Oh! almighty Zeus! see to it that the gods protect us, albeit we are but women!

WOMAN HERALD: Hearken, all of you! this is the decree passed by the Senate of the Women under the presidency of Timoclea and at the suggestion of Sostrate; it is signed by Lysilla, the secretary: "There will be a gathering of the people on the morning of the third day of the Thesmophoria, which is a day of rest for us; the principal business there shall be the punishment that it is meet to inflict upon Euripides for the insults with which he has loaded us." Now who asks to speak?

FIRST WOMAN: I do.

WOMAN HERALD: First put on this garland, and then speak.

LEADER OF THE CHORUS: Silence! let all be quiet! Pay attention! for here she is spitting as orators generally do before they begin; no doubt she has much to say.

FIRST WOMAN: If I have asked to speak, may the goddesses bear me witness, it was not for sake of ostentation. But I have long been pained to see us women insulted by this Euripides, this son of the green-stuff woman, who loads us with every kind of indignity. Has he not hit us enough, calumniated us sufficiently, wherever there are spectators, tragedians, and a chorus? Does; he not style us adulterous, lecherous, bibulous, treacherous, and garrulous? Does he not repeat that we are all vice, that we are the curse of our husbands? So that, directly they come back from the theatre, they look at us doubtfully and go searching every nook, fearing there may be some hidden lover. We can do nothing as we used to, so many are the false ideas which he has instilled into our husbands. Is a woman weaving a garland for herself? It's because she is in love. Does she let some vase drop while going or returning to the house? her husband asks her in whose honour she has broken it: "It can only be for that Corinthian stranger." Is a maiden unwell? Straightway her brother says, "That is a colour that does not please me." And if a childless woman wishes to substitute one, the deceit can no longer be a secret, for the neighbours will insist on being present at her delivery. Formerly the old men married young girls, but they have been so calumniated that none think of them now, thanks to that line of his: "A woman is the tyrant of the old man who marries her." Again, it is because of Euripides that we are incessantly watched, that we are shut up behind bolts and bars, and that dogs are kept to frighten off the adulterers. Let that pass; but formerly it was we who had the care of the food, who fetched the flour from the storeroom, the oil and the wine; we can do it no more. Our husbands now carry little Spartan keys on their persons, made with three notches and full of malice and spite. Formerly it sufficed to purchase a ring marked with the same sign for three obols, to open the most securely sealed-up door! but now this pestilent Euripides has taught men to hang seals of worm-eaten wood about their necks. My opinion, therefore, is that we should rid ourselves of our enemy by poison or by any other means, provided he dies. That is what I announce publicly; as to certain points, which I wish to keep secret, I propose to record them on the secretary's minutes.

CHORUS: [singing] Never have I listened to a cleverer or more eloquent woman. Everything she says is true; she has examined the matter from all sides and has weighed up every detail. Her arguments are close, varied, and happily chosen. I believe that Xenocles himself, the son of Carcinus, would seem to talk mere nonsense, if placed beside her.

SECOND WOMAN: I have only a very few words to add, for the last speaker has covered the various points of the indictment; allow me only to tell you what happened to me. My husband died at Cyprus, leaving me five children, whom I had great trouble to bring up by weaving chaplets on the myrtle market. Anyhow, I lived as well as I could until this wretch had persuaded the spectators by his tragedies that there were no gods; since then I have not sold as many chaplets by half. I charge you therefore and exhort you all to punish him, for does he not deserve it in a thousand respects, he who loads you with troubles, who is as coarse toward you as the vegetables upon which his mother reared him? But I must back to the market to weave my chaplets; I have twenty to deliver yet.

CHORUS: [singing] This is even more animated and more trenchant than the first speech; all she has just said is full of good sense and to the point; it is clever, clear and well calculated to convince. Yes! we must have striking vengeance on the insults of Euripides.

MNESILOCHUS: Oh, women! I am not astonished at these outbursts of fiery rage; how could your bile not get inflamed against Euripides, who has spoken so ill of you? As for myself, I hate the man, I swear it by my children; it would be madness not to hate him! Yet, let us reflect a little; we are alone and our words will not be repeated outside. Why be so bent on his ruin? Because he has known and shown up two or three of our faults, when we have a thousand? As for myself, not to speak of other women, I have more than one great sin upon my conscience, but this is the blackest of them. I had been married three days and my husband was asleep by my side; I had a lover, who had seduced me when I was seven years old; impelled by his passion, he came scratching at the door; I understood at once he was there and was going down noiselessly. "Where are you going?" asked my husband. "I am suffering terribly with colic," I told him, "and am going to the can." "Go ahead," he replied, and started pounding together juniper berries, aniseed, and sage. As for myself, I moistened the door-hinge and went to find my lover, who laid me, half-reclining upon Apollo's altar and holding on to the sacred laurel with one hand. Well now! Consider! that is a thing of which Euripides has never spoken. And when we bestow our favours on slaves and muleteers for want of better, does he mention this? And when we eat garlic early in the morning after a night of wantonness, so that our husband, who has been keeping guard upon the city wall, may be reassured by the smell and suspect nothing, has Euripides ever breathed a word of this? Tell me. Neither has he spoken of the woman who spreads open a large cloak before her husband's eyes to make him admire it in full daylight to conceal her lover by so doing and afford him the means of making his escape. I know another, who for ten whole days pretended to be suffering the pains of labour until she had secured a child; the husband hurried in all directions to buy drugs to hasten her deliverance, and meanwhile an old woman brought the infant in a stew-pot; to prevent its crying she had stopped up its mouth with honey. With a sign she told the wife that she was bringing a child for her, who at once began exclaiming, "Go away, friend, go away, I think I am going to be delivered; I can feel him kicking his heels in the belly ....of the stew-pot." The husband goes off full of joy, and the old wretch quickly takes the honey out of the child's mouth, which starts crying; then she seizes the baby, runs to the father and tells him with a smile on her face, "It's a lion, a lion, that is born to you; it's your very image. Everything about it is like you, even his little tool, curved like the sky." Are these not our everyday tricks?

Why certainly, by Artemis, and we, are angry with Euripides, who assuredly treats us no worse than we deserve!

CHORUS: [singing] Great gods! where has she unearthed all that? What country gave birth to such an audacious woman? Oh! you wretch! I should not have thought ever a one of us could have spoken in public with such impudence. 'Tis clear, however, that we must expect everything and, as the old proverb says, must look beneath every stone, lest it conceal some orator ready to sting us.

LEADER OF THE CHORUS: There is but one thing in the world worse than a shameless woman, and that's another woman.

FIRST WOMAN: By Aglaurus! you have lost your wits, friends! You must be bewitched to suffer this plague to belch forth insults against us all. Is there no one has any spirit at all? If not, we and our maid-servants will punish her. Run and fetch coals and let's depilate her in proper style, to teach her not to speak ill of her sex.

MNESILOCHUS: Oh no no! not that part of me, my friends. Have we not the right to speak frankly at this gathering? And because I have uttered what I thought right in favour of Euripides, do you want to depilate me for my trouble?

FIRST WOMAN What! we ought not to punish you, who alone have dared to defend the man who has done so much harm, whom it pleases to put all the vile women that ever were upon the stage, who only shows us Melanippes and Phaedras? But of Penelope he has never said a word, because she was reputed chaste and good.

MNESILOCHUS: I know the reason. It's because not a single Penelope exists among the women of to-day, but all without exception are Phaedras.

FIRST WOMAN: Women, you hear how this creature still dares to speak of us all.

MNESILOCHUS: And, Heaven knows, I have not said all that I know. Do you want any more?

FIRST WOMAN: You cannot tell us any more; you have crapped out all you know.

MNESILOCHUS: Why, I have not told the thousandth part of what we women do. Have I said how we use the hollow bandles of our brooms to draw up wine unbeknown to our husbands?

FIRST WOMAN: The cursed jade!

MNESILOCHUS: And how we give meats to our pimps at the feast of the Apaturia and then accuse the cat....

FIRST WOMAN: You're crazy!

MNESILOCHUS: ....Have I mentioned the woman who killed her husband with a hatchet? Of another, who caused hers to lose his reason with her potions? And of the Acharnian woman....

FIRST WOMAN: Die, you bitch!

MNESILOCHUS: ....who buried her father beneath the bath?

FIRST WOMAN: And yet we listen to such things!

MNESILOCHUS: Have I told how you attributed to yourself the male child your slave had just borne and gave her your little daughter?

FIRST WOMAN: This insult calls for vengeance. Look out for your hair!

MNESILOCHUS: By Zeus! don't touch me.

FIRST WOMAN: [slapping him] There!

MNESILOCHUS: [hitting back] There! tit for tat!

FIRST WOMAN: Hold my cloak, Philista!

MNESILOCHUS: Come on then, and by Demeter....

FIRST WOMAN: Well! what?

MNESILOCHUS: I'll make you crap forth the sesame-cake you have eaten.

LEADER OF THE CHORUS: Stop wrangling! I see a woman running here in hot haste. Keep silent, so that we may hear the better what she has to say. [Enter CLISTHENES, dressed as a woman.]

CLISTHENES: Friends, whom I copy in all things, my hairless chin sufficiently evidences how dear you are to me; I am women-mad and make myself their champion wherever I am. Just now on the market-place I heard mention of a thing that is of the greatest importance to you; I come to tell it to you, to let you know it, so that you may watch carefully and be on your guard against the danger which threatens you.

LEADER OF THE CHORUS: What is it, my child? I can well call you child, for you have so smooth a skin.

CLISTHENES: They say that Euripides has sent an old man here to-day, one of his relations....

LEADER OF THE CHORUS: With what object? What is his idea?

CLISTHENES: ....so that he may hear your speeches and inform him of your deliberations and intentions.

LEADER OF THE CHORUS: But how would a man fail to be recognized amongst women?

CLISTHENES: Euripides singed and depilated him and disguised him as a woman.

MNESILOCHUS: This is pure invention! What man is fool enough to let himself be depilated? As for myself, I don't believe a word of it.

CLISTHENES: Nonsense! I should not have come here to tell you, if I did not know it on indisputable authority.

LEADER OF THE CHORUS: Great gods! what is it you tell us! Come, women, let us not lose a moment; let us search and rummage everywhere! Where can this man have hidden himself to escape our notice? Help us to look, Clisthenes; we shall thus owe you double thanks, dear friend.

CLISTHENES: Well then! let us see. To begin with you; who are you?

MNESILOCHUS: [aside] Wherever am I to stow myself?

CLISTHENES: Each and every one must pass the scrutiny.

MNESILOCHUS: [aside] Oh! great gods!

FIRST WOMAN: You ask me who I am? I am the wife of Cleonynus.

CLISTHENES: [to the LEADER OF THE CHORUS] Do you know this woman?

LEADER OF THE CHORUS: Yes, yes, pass on to the rest.

CLISTHENES: And she who carries the child?

FIRST WOMAN: Surely; she's my nurse.

MNESILOCHUS: [aside] This is the end. [He runs off.]

CLISTHENES: Hi! you there! where are you going? Stop. What are you running away for?

MNESILOCHUS: [dancing on one leg] I want to take a pee, you brazen thing.

CLISTHENES: Well, be quick about it; I shall wait for you here.

LEADER OF THE CHORUS: Wait for her and examine her closely; she's the only one we do not know.

CLISTHENES: That's a long leak you're taking.

MNESILOCHUS: God, yes; I am constricted; I ate some cress yesterday.

CLISTHENES: What are you chattering about cress? Come here! and be quick. [He starts to pull MNESILOCHUS: back.]

MNESILOCHUS: Oh! don't pull a poor sick woman about like that.

CLISTHENES: [looking MNESILOCHUS: square in the eye] Tell me, who is your husband?

MNESILOCHUS: [embarrassed] My husband? Do you know a certain individual at Cothocidae...?

CLISTHENES: Whom do you mean? Give his name.

MNESILOCHUS: He's an individual to whom the son of a certain individual one day...

CLISTHENES: You are drivelling! Let's see, have you ever been here before?

MNESILOCHUS: Why certainly, every year.

CLISTHENES: Who is your tent companion?

MNESILOCHUS: A certain.... Oh! my god!

CLISTHENES: That's not an answer!

FIRST WOMAN: Withdraw, all of you; I am going to examine her thoroughly about last year's mysteries. But move away, Clisthenes, for no man may hear what is going to be said. Now answer my questions! What was done first?

MNESILOCHUS: Let's see now. What was done first? Oh! we drank.

FIRST WOMAN: And then?

MNESILOCHUS: We drank to our healths.

FIRST WOMAN: You will have heard that from someone. And then?

MNESILOCHUS: Xenylla asked for a cup; there wasn't any thunder-mug.

FIRST WOMAN: You're talking nonsense. Here, Clisthenes, here This is the man you were telling us about.

CLISTHENES: What shall we do with him?

FIRST WOMAN: Take off his clothes, I can get nothing out of him.

MNESILOCHUS: What! are you going to strip a mother of nine children naked?

CLISTHENES: Come, undo your girdle, you shameless thing.

FIRST WOMAN: Ah! what a sturdy frame! but she has no breasts like we have.

MNESILOCHUS: That's because I'm barren. I never had any children.

FIRST WOMAN: Oh! indeed! just now you were the mother of nine.

CLISTHENES: Stand up straight. What do you keep pushing that thing down for?

FIRST WOMAN: [peering from behind] There's no mistaking it.

CLISTHENES: [also peering from behind] Where has it gone to now?

FIRST WOMAN: To the front.

CLISTHENES: [from in front] No.

FIRST WOMAN: [from behind] Ah! it's behind now.

CLISTHENES: Why, friend, it's just like the Isthmus; you keep pulling your stick backwards and forwards more often than the Corinthians do their ships

FIRST WOMAN: Ah! the wretch! this is why he insulted us and defended Euripides.

MNESILOCHUS: Aye, wretch indeed, what troubles have I not got into now!

FIRST WOMAN: What shall we do?

CLISTHENES: Watch him closely, so that he does not escape. As for me, I'll go to report the matter to the magistrates.

LEADER OF THE CHORUS: Let us kindle our lamps; let us go firmly to work and with courage, let us take off our cloaks and search whether some other man has not come here too; let us pass round the whole Pnyx, examine the tents and the passages. Come, be quick, let us start off on a light toe and rummage all round in silence. Let us hasten, let us finish our round as soon as possible.

CHORUS: [singing] Look quickly for the traces that might show you a man hidden here, let your glance fall on every side; look well to the right and to the left. If we seize some impious fellow, woe to him! He will know how we punish the outrage, the crime, the sacrilege. The criminal will then acknowledge at last that gods exist; his fate will teach all men that the deities must be revered, that justice must be observed and that they must submit to the sacred laws. If not, then woe to them! Heaven itself will punish sacrilege; being aflame with fury and mad with frenzy, all their deeds will prove to mortals, both men and women, that the deity punishes injustice and impiety, and that she is not slow to strike.

LEADER OF THE CHORUS: But I think I have now searched everywhere and that no other man is hidden among us.

FIRST WOMAN: Where are you flying to? Stop! stop! Ah! miserable woman that I am, he has torn my child from my breast and has disappeared with it.

MNESILOCHUS: Scream as loud as you will, but you'll never feed him again. If you do not let me go this very instant, I am going to cut open the veins of his thighs with this cutlass and his blood shall flow over the altar.

FIRST WOMAN: Oh! great gods! oh! friends, help me! terrify him with your shrieks, triumph over this monster, permit him not to rob me of my only child.

LEADER OF THE CHORUS: Oh! oh! venerable Moirai, what fresh attack is this? It's the crowning act of audacity and shamelessness! What has he done now, friends, what has he done?

MNESILOCHUS: Ah! your insolence passes all bounds, but I know how to curb it!

LEADER OF THE CHORUS: What a shameful deed! the measure of his iniquities is full!

FIRST WOMAN: Aye, it's shameful that he should have robbed me of my child.

CHORUS: [singing] It's past belief to be so criminal and so impudent!

MNESILOCHUS: [singing] Ah! you're not near the end of it yet.

CHORUS: [singing] Little I care whence you come; you shall not return to boast of having acted so odiously with impunity, for you shall be punished.

MNESILOCHUS: [speaking] You won't do it, by the gods!

CHORUS: [singing] And what immortal would protect you for your crime?

MNESILOCHUS: [speaking] You talk in vain! I shall not let go the child.

CHORUS: [singing] By the goddesses, you will not laugh presently over your crime and your impious speech. For with impiety, as 'tis meet, shall we reply to your impiety. Soon fortune will turn round and overwhelm you.

LEADER OF THE CHORUS: Come there, bring some firewood. Let's roast the wretch as quickly as we can.

FIRST WOMAN: Bring faggots, Mania! [To MNESILOCHUS:] You will be nothing but charcoal soon.

MNESILOCHUS: Grill away, roast me, but you, my child, take off this Cretan robe and blame no one but your mother for your death. But what does this mean? The little girl is nothing but a skin filled with wine and shod with Persian slippers. Oh! you wanton, you tippling women, who think of nothing but wine; you are a fortune to the drinking-shops and are our ruin; for the sake of drink, you neglect both your household and your shuttle!

FIRST WOMAN: Faggots, Mania, plenty of them.

MNESILOCHUS: Bring as many as you like. But answer me; are you the mother of this brat?

FIRST WOMAN: I carried it ten months.

MNESILOCHUS: You carried it?

FIRST WOMAN: I swear it by Artemis.

MNESILOCHUS: How much does it hold? Three cotylae? Tell me.

FIRST WOMAN: Oh! what have you done? You have stripped the poor child quite naked, and it is so small, so small.

MNESILOCHUS: So small?

FIRST WOMAN: Yes, quite small, to be sure.

MNESILOCHUS: How old is it? Has it seen the feast of cups thrice or four times?

FIRST WOMAN: It was born about the time of the last Dionysia. But give it back to me.

MNESILOCHUS: No, may Apollo bear me witness.

FIRST WOMAN: Well, then we are going to burn him.

MNESILOCHUS: Burn me, but then I shall rip this open instantly.

FIRST WOMAN: No, no, I adjure you, don't; do anything you like to me rather than that.

MNESILOCHUS: What a tender mother you are; but nevertheless I shall rip it open. [He tears open the wine-skin.]

FIRST WOMAN: Oh, my beloved daughter! Mania, hand me the sacred cup, that I may at least catch the blood of my child.

MNESILOCHUS: Hold it below; that's the only favour I grant you. [He pours the wine into the cup.]

FIRST WOMAN: Out upon you, you pitiless monster!

MNESILOCHUS: This robe belongs to the priestess.

SECOND WOMAN What belongs to the priestess?

MNESILOCHUS: Here, take it. [He throws her the Cretan robe.]

SECOND WOMAN Ah! unfortunate Mica! Who has robbed you of your daughter, your beloved child?

FIRST WOMAN: That wretch. But as you are here, watch him well, while I go with Clisthenes to the Magistrates and denounce him for his crimes.

MNESILOCHUS: Ah! how can I secure safety? what device can I hit on? what can I think of? He whose fault it is, he who hurried me into this trouble, will not come to my rescue. Let me see, whom could I best send to him? Ha! I know a means taken from Palamedes; like him, I will write my misfortune on some oars, which I will cast into the sea. Where might I find some oars? Hah! what if I took these statues instead of oars, wrote upon them and then threw them towards this side and that. That's the best thing to do. Besides, like oars they are of wood. [singing] Oh! my hands, keep up your courage, for my safety is at stake. Come, my beautiful tablets, receive the traces of my stylus and be the messengers of my sorry fate. Oh! oh! this R looks miserable enough! Where is it running to then? Come, off with you in all directions, to the right and to the left; and hurry yourselves, for there's much need indeed! [He sits down to wait for Euripides. The Chorus turns and faces the audience.]

LEADER OF THE CHORUS: Let us address ourselves to the spectators to sing our praises, despite the fact that each one says much ill of women. If the men are to be believed, we are a plague to them;

through us come all their troubles, quarrels, disputes, sedition, griefs and wars. But if we are truly such a pest, why marry us? Why forbid us to go out or show ourselves at the window? You want to keep this pest, and take a thousand cares to do it. If your wife goes out and you meet her away from the house, you fly into a fury. Ought you not rather to rejoice and give thanks to the gods? for if the pest has disappeared, you will no longer find it at home. If we fall asleep at friends' houses from the fatigue of playing and sporting, each of you comes prowling round the bed to contemplate the features of this pest. If we seat ourselves at the window, each one wants to see the pest, and if we withdraw through modesty, each wants all the more to see the pest perch herself there again. It is thus clear that we are better than you, and the proof of this is easy. Let us find out which is the worse of the two sexes. We say, "It's you," while you aver, "it's we."' Come, let us compare them in detail, each individual man with a woman. Charminus is not equal to Nausimache, that's certain. Cleophon is in every respect inferior to Salabaccho. It's a long time now since any of you has dared to contest the prize with Aristomache, the heroine of Marathon, or with Stratonice.

Among the last year's Senators, who have just yielded their office to other citizens, is there one who equals Eubule? Not even Anytus would say that. Therefore we maintain that men are greatly our inferiors. You see no woman who has robbed the state of fifty talents rushing about the city in a magnificent chariot; our greatest peculations are a measure of corn, which we steal from our husbands, and even then we return it to them the very same day. But we could name many amongst you who do quite as much, and who are, even more than ourselves, gluttons, parasites, cheats and kidnappers of slaves. We know how to keep our property better than you. We still have our cylinders, our beams, our baskets and our surshades; whereas many among you have lost the wood of your spears as well as the iron, and many others have cast away their bucklers on the battlefield.

There are many reproaches we have the right to bring against men. The most serious is this, that the woman, who has given birth to a useful citizen, whether taxiarch or strategus should receive some distinction; a place of honour should be reserved for her at the Stenia, the Scirophoria, and the other festivals that we keep. On the other hand, she of whom a coward was born or a worthless man, a bad trierarch or an unskilful pilot, should sit with shaven head, behind her sister who had borne a brave man. Oh! citizens! is it just that the mother of Hyperbolus should sit dressed in white and with loosened tresses beside that of Lamachus and lend out money on usury? He, who may have made a deal of this nature with her, so far from paying her interest, should not even repay the capital, saying, "What, pay you interest? after you have given us this delightful son?"

MNESILOCHUS: I have contracted quite a squint by looking round for him, and yet Euripides does not come. Who is keeping him? No doubt he is ashamed of his cold Palamedes. What will attract him? Let us see! By which of his pieces does he set most store? Ah! I'll imitate his Helen, his last-born. I just happen to have a complete woman's outfit.

SECOND WOMAN What are you ruminating about now? Why are you rolling up your eyes? You'll have no reason to be proud of your Helen, if you don't keep quiet until one of the Magistrates arrives.

MNESILOCHUS: [as Helen] "These shores are those of the Nile with the beautiful nymphs, these waters take the place of heaven's rain and fertilize the white earth, that produces the black syrmea."

SECOND WOMAN By bright Hecate, you're a cunning varlet.

MNESILOCHUS: "Glorious Sparta is my country and Tyndareus is my father."

SECOND WOMAN He your father, you rascal! Why, it's Phrynondas.

MNESILOCHUS: "I was given the name of Helen."

SECOND WOMAN What! you are again becoming a woman, before we have punished you for having pretended it the first time?

MNESILOCHUS: "A thousand warriors have died on my account on the banks of the Scamander."

SECOND WOMAN Would that you had done the same!

MNESILOCHUS: "And here I am upon these shores; Menelaus, my unhappy husband, does not yet come. Ah! Why do I still live?"

SECOND WOMAN Because of the criminal negligence of the crows!

MNESILOCHUS: "But what sweet hope is this that sets my heart a-throb? Oh, Zeus! grant it may not prove a lying one!" [EURIPIDES enters.]

EURIPIDES: [as Menelaus] "To what master does this splendid palace belong? Will he welcome strangers who have been tried on the billows of the sea by storm and shipwreck?"

MNESILOCHUS: "This is the palace of Proteus."

SECOND WOMAN Of what Proteus? you thrice cursed rascal! how he lies! By the goddesses, it's ten years since Proteas died.

EURIPIDES: "What is this shore whither the wind has driven our boat?"

MNESILOCHUS: "'Tis Egypt."

EURIPIDES: "Alas! how far we are from own country!

SECOND WOMAN Don't believe that cursed fool. This is Demeter's Temple.

EURIPIDES: "Is Proteus in these parts?"

SECOND WOMAN Ah, now, stranger, it must be sea-sickness that makes you so distraught! You have been told that

Proteas is dead, and yet you ask if he is in these parts.

EURIPIDES: "He is no more! Oh! woe! where lie his ashes?"

MNESILOCHUS: "'Tis on his tomb you see me sitting."

SECOND WOMAN You call an altar a tomb! Beware of the rope!

EURIPIDES: "And why remain sitting on this tomb, wrapped in this long veil, oh, stranger lady?"

MNESILOCHUS: "They want to force me to marry a son of Proteus."

SECOND WOMAN Ah! wretch, why tell such shameful lies? Stranger, this is a rascal who has slipped in amongst us women to rob us of our trinkets.

MNESILOCHUS: [to SECOND WOMAN] "Shout! load me with your insults, for little care I."

EURIPIDES: "Who is the old woman who reviles you, stranger lady?

MNESILOCHUS: "'Tis Theonoe, the daughter of Proteus."

SECOND WOMAN I! Why, my name's Critylle, the daughter of Antitheus, of the deme of Gargettus; as for you, you are a rogue.

MNESILOCHUS: "Your entreaties are vain. Never shall I wed your brother; never shall I betray the faith I owe my husband, Menelaus, who is fighting before Troy."

EURIPIDES: "What are you saying? Turn your face towards me."

MNESILOCHUS: "I dare not; my cheeks show the marks of the insults I have been forced to suffer."

EURIPIDES: "Oh! great gods! I cannot speak, for very emotion.... Ah! what do I see? Who are you?"

MNESILOCHUS: "And you, what is your name? for my surprise is as great as yours."

EURIPIDES: "Are you Grecian or born in this country?"

MNESILOCHUS: "I am Grecian. But now your name, what is it?"

EURIPIDES: "Oh how you resemble Helen!

MNESILOCHUS: "And you Menelaus, if I can judge by these pot-herbs."

EURIPIDES: "You are not mistaken, 'tis none other than that unfortunate mortal who stands before you."

MNESILOCHUS: "Ah! how you have delayed coming to your wife's arms! Press me to your heart, throw your arms about me, for I wish to cover you with kisses. Carry me away, carry me away, quick, quick, far, very far from here."

SECOND WOMAN By the goddesses, woe to him who would carry you away! I should thrash him with my torch.

EURIPIDES: "Do you propose to prevent me from taking my wife, the daughter of Tyndareus, to Sparta?"

SECOND WOMAN You seem to me to be a cunning rascal too; you are in collusion with this man, and it wasn't for nothing that you kept babbling about Egypt. But the hour for punishment has come; here is the Magistrate with his Scythian.

EURIPIDES: This is getting awkward. Let me hide myself.

MNESILOCHUS: And what is to become of me, poor unfortunate man that I am?

EURIPIDES: Don't worry. I shall never abandon you, as long as I draw breath and one of my numberless artifices remains untried.

MNESILOCHUS: The fish has not bitten this time. [A MAGISTRATE enters, accompanied by a Scythian policeman.]

MAGISTRATE: Is this the rascal Clisthenes told us about? Why are you trying to make yourself so small? Officer, arrest him, fasten him to the post, then take up your position there and keep guard over him. Let none approach him. A sound lash with your whip for him who attempts to break the order.

SECOND WOMAN Excellent, for just now a rogue almost took him from me.

MNESILOCHUS: Magistrate, in the name of that hand which you know so well how to bend when money is placed in it, grant me a slight favour before I die.

MAGISTRATE: What favour?

MNESILOCHUS: Order the archer to strip me before lashing me to the post; the crows, when they make their meal on the poor old man, would laugh too much at this robe and head-dress,

MAGISTRATE: It is in that gear that you must be exposed by order of the Senate, so that your crime may be patent to the passers-by. [He departs.]

MNESILOCHUS: [as the SCYTHIAN seizes him] Oh! cursed robe, the cause of all my misfortune! My last hope is thus destroyed!

LEADER OF THE CHORUS: Let us now devote ourselves to the sports which the women are accustomed to celebrate here, when time has again brought round the mighty Mysteries of the great goddesses, the sacred days which Pauson himself honours by fasting and would wish feast to succeed feast, that he might keep them all holy. Spring forward with a light step, whirling in mazy circles; let your hands interlace, let the eager and rapid dancers sway to the music and glance on every side as they move.

CHORUS: [singing] Let the chorus sing likewise and praise the Olympian gods in their pious transport. It's wrong to suppose that, because I am a woman and in this temple, I am going to speak ill of men; but since we want something fresh, we are going through the rhythmic steps of the round dance for the first time.

Start off while you sing to the god of the lyre and to the chaste goddess armed with the bow. Hail I thou god who flingest thy darts so far, grant us the victory! The homage of our song is also due to Here, the goddess of marriage, who interests herself in every chorus and guards the approach to the nuptial couch. I also pray Hermes, the god of the shepherds, and Pan and the beloved Graces to bestow a benevolent smile upon our songs.

Let us lead off anew, let us double our zeal during our solemn days, and especially let us observe a close fast; let us form fresh measures that keep good time, and may our songs resound to the very heavens. Do thou, oh divine Bacchus, who art crowned with ivy, direct our chorus; 'tis to thee that both my hymns and my dances are dedicated; oh, Evius, oh, Bromius, oh, thou son of Semeld, oh, Bacchus, who delightest to mingle with the dear choruses of the nymphs upon the mountains, and who repeatest, while dancing with them, the sacred hymn, Euios, Euios, Euoi! Echo, the nymph of Cithaeron, returns thy words, which resound beneath the dark vaults of the thick foliage and in the midst of the rocks of the forest; the ivy enlaces thy brow with its tendrils charged with flowers.

SCYTHIAN: [he speaks with a heavy foreign accent] You shall stay here in the open air to wail.

MNESILOCHUS: Archer, I adjure you.

SCYTHIAN: You're wasting your breath.

MNESILOCHUS: Loosen the wedge a little.

SCYTHIAN: Aye, certainly.

MNESILOCHUS: Oh by the gods! why, you are driving it in tighter.

SCYTHIAN: Is that enough?

MNESILOCHUS: Oh! Oh! Ow! Ow! May the plague take you!

SCYTHIAN: Silence! you cursed old wretch! I am going to get a mat to lie upon, so as to watch you close at hand at my ease.

MNESILOCHUS: Ah! what exquisite pleasures Euripides is securing for me! But, oh, ye gods! oh, Zeus the Deliverer, all is not yet lost! I don't believe him the man to break his word; I just caught sight of him appearing in the form of Perseus, and he told me with a mysterious sign to turn myself into Andromeda. And in truth am I not really bound? It's certain, then, that be is coming to my rescue; for otherwise he would not have steered his flight this way. [As Andromeda, singing] Oh Nymphs, ye virgins who are so dear to me, how am I to approach him? how can I escape the sight of this Scythian? And Echo, thou who reignest in the inmost recesses of the caves, oh! favour my cause and permit me to approach my spouse. A pitiless ruffian has chained up the most unfortunate of mortal maids. Alas! I bad barely escaped the filthy claws of an old fury, when another mischance overtook me! This Scythian does not take his eye off me and he has exposed me as food for the crows. Alas! what is to become of me, alone here and without friends! I am not seen mingling in the dances nor in the games of my companions, but heavily loaded with fetters I am given over to the voracity of a Glaucetes. Sing no bridal hymn for me, oh women, but rather the hymn of captivity, and in tears. Ah! how I suffer! great gods! how I suffer! Alas! alas! and through my own relatives too! My misery would make Tartarus dissolve into tears! Alas! in my terrible distress, I implore the mortal who first shaved me and depilated me, then dressed me in this long robe, and then sent me to this Temple into the midst of the women, to save me. Oh! thou pitiless Fate! I am then accursed, great gods! Ah! who would not be moved at the sight of the appalling tortures under which I succumb? Would that the blazing shaft of the lightning would wither.... this barbarian for me! The immortal light has no further charm for my eyes since I have been descending the shortest path to the dead, tied up, strangled, and maddened with pain. [In the following scene EURIPIDES, from off stage, impersonates Echo.]

EURIPIDES: Hail! beloved girl. As for your father, Cepheus, who has exposed you in this guise, may the gods annihilate him.

MNESILOCHUS: And who are you whom my misfortunes have moved to pity?

EURIPIDES: I am Echo, the nymph who repeats all she hears. It was I, who last year lent my help to Euripides in this very place. But, my child, give yourself up to the sad laments that belong to your pitiful condition.

MNESILOCHUS: And you will repeat them?

EURIPIDES: I will not fail you. Begin.

MNESILOCHUS: [singing] "Oh! thou divine Night! how slowly thy chariot threads its way through the starry vault, across the sacred realms of the Air and mighty Olympus."

EURIPIDES: [singing] Mighty Olympus.

MNESILOCHUS: [singing] "Why is it necessary that Andromeda should have all the woes for her share?

EURIPIDES: [singing] For her share.

MNESILOCHUS: [speaking] "Sad death!

EURIPIDES: Sad death!

MNESILOCHUS: You weary me, old babbler.

EURIPIDES: Old babbler.

MNESILOCHUS: Oh! you are too unbearable.

EURIPIDES: Unbearable.

MNESILOCHUS: Friend, let me talk by myself. Do please let me. Come, that's enough.

EURIPIDES: That's enough.

MNESILOCHUS: Go and hang yourself!

EURIPIDES: Go and hang yourself!

MNESILOCHUS: What a plague!

EURIPIDES: What a plague!

MNESILOCHUS: Cursed brute!

EURIPIDES: Cursed brute!

MNESILOCHUS: Beware of blows!

EURIPIDES: Beware of blows!

SCYTHIAN: Hullo! what are you jabbering about?

EURIPIDES: What are you jabbering about?

SCYTHIAN: I shall go and call the Magistrates.

EURIPIDES: I shall go and call the Magistrates.

SCYTHIAN: This is odd!

EURIPIDES: This is odd!

SCYTHIAN: Whence comes this voice?

EURIPIDES: Whence comes this voice?

SCYTHIAN: You are mad.

EURIPIDES: You are mad.

SCYTHIAN: Ah! beware!

EURIPIDES: Ah! beware!

SCYTHIAN: [to MNESILOCHUS:] Are you mocking me?

EURIPIDES: Are you mocking me?

MNESILOCHUS: No, it's this woman, who stands near you.

EURIPIDES: Who stands near you.

SCYTHIAN: Where is the hussy!

MNESILOCHUS: She's running away.

SCYTHIAN: Where are you running to?

EURIPIDES: Where are you running to?

SCYTHIAN: You shall not get away.

EURIPIDES: You shall not get away.

SCYTHIAN: You are chattering still?

EURIPIDES: You are chattering still?

SCYTHIAN: Stop the hussy.

EURIPIDES: Stop the hussy.

SCYTHIAN: What a babbling, cursed woman! [EURIPIDES now enters, costumed as Perseus.]

EURIPIDES: "Oh! ye gods! to what barbarian land has my swift flight taken me? I am Perseus; I cleave the plains of the air with my winged feet, and I am carrying the Gorgon's head to Argos."

SCYTHIAN: What, are you talking about the head of Gorgos, the scribe?

EURIPIDES: No, I am speaking of the head of the Gorgon.

SCYTHIAN: Why, yes! of Gorgos!

EURIPIDES: "But what do I behold? A young maiden, beautiful as the immortals, chained to this rock like a vessel in port?"

MNESILOCHUS: "Take pity on me, oh stranger! I am so unhappy and distraught! Free me from these bonds."

SCYTHIAN: You keep still! a curse upon your impudence! you are going to die, and yet you will be chattering!

EURIPIDES: "Oh! virgin! I take pity on your chains."

SCYTHIAN: But this is no virgin; he's an old rogue, a cheat and a thief.

EURIPIDES: You have lost your wits, SCYTHIAN. This is Andromeda, the daughter of Cepheus.

SCYTHIAN: [lifting up MNESILOCHUS:' robe] But look at his tool; it's pretty big.

EURIPIDES: Give me your hand, that I may descend near this young maiden. Each man has his own particular weakness; as for me I am aflame with love for this virgin.

SCYTHIAN: Oh! I'm not jealous; and as he has his arse turned this way, why, I don't care if you make love to him.

EURIPIDES: "Ah! let me release her, and hasten to join her on the bridal couch."

SCYTHIAN: If you are so eager to make the old man, you can bore through the plank, and so get at him.

EURIPIDES: No, I will break his bonds.

SCYTHIAN: Beware of my lash!

EURIPIDES: No matter.

SCYTHIAN: This blade shall cut off your head.

EURIPIDES: "Ah! what can be done? what arguments can I use? This savage will understand nothing! The newest and most cunning fancies are a dead letter to the ignorant. Let us invent some artifice to fit in with his coarse nature." [He departs.]

SCYTHIAN: I can see the rascal is trying to outwit me.

MNESILOCHUS: Ah! Perseus! remember in what condition you are leaving me.

SCYTHIAN: Are you wanting to feel my lash again!

CHORUS: [singing] Oh! Pallas, who art fond of dances, hasten hither at my call. Oh! thou chaste virgin, the protectress of Athens, I call thee in accordance with the sacred rites, thee, whose evident protection we adore and who keepest the keys of our city in thy hands. Do thou appear, thou whose just hatred has overturned our tyrants. The womenfolk are calling thee; hasten hither at their bidding along with Peace, who shall restore the festivals. And ye, august goddesses, display a smiling and propitious countenance to our gaze; come into your sacred grove, the entry to which is forbidden to men; 'tis there in the midst of the sacred orgies that we contemplate your divine features. Come, appear, we pray it of you, oh, venerable Thesmophorae! Is you have ever answered our appeal, oh! come into our midst. [During this ode the SCYTHIAN falls asleep. At the end of it EURIPIDES returns, thinly disguised as an old procuress; the CHORUS recognizes him, the SCYTHIAN does not; he carries a harp, and is followed by a dancing girl and a young flute-girl.]

EURIPIDES: Women, if you will be reconciled with me, I am willing, and I undertake never to say anything ill of you in future. Those are my proposals for peace.

LEADER OF THE CHORUS: And what impels you to make these overtures?

EURIPIDES: [to the CHORUS] This unfortunate man, who is chained to the post, is my father-in-law; if you will restore him to me, you will have no more cause to complain of me; but if not, I shall reveal your pranks to your husbands when they return from the war.

LEADER OF THE CHORUS: We accept peace, but there is this barbarian whom you must buy over.

EURIPIDES: I'll take care of that. Come, my little wench, bear in mind what I told you on the road and do it well. Come, go past him and gird up your robe. And you, you little dear, play us the air of a Persian dance.

SCYTHIAN: [waking] What is this music that makes me so blithe?

EURIPIDES: Scythian, this young girl is going to practise some dances, which she has to perform at a feast presently.

SCYTHIAN: Very well! let her dance and practise; I won't hinder her. How nimbly she bounds! just like a flea on a fleece.

EURIPIDES: Come, my dear, off with your robe and seat yourself on the Scythian's knee; stretch forth your feet to me, that I may take off your slippers.

SCYTHIAN: Ah! yes, seat yourself, my little girl, ah! yes, to be sure. What a firm little titty! it's just like a turnip.

EURIPIDES: [to the flute-girl] An air on the flute, quick! Are you afraid of the Scythian?

SCYTHIAN: What a nice arse! Hold still, won't you? A nice twat, too.

EURIPIDES: That's so! [To the dancing girl] Resume your dress, it is time to be going.

SCYTHIAN: Give me a kiss.

EURIPIDES: Come, give him a kiss.

SCYTHIAN: Oh! oh! oh! my god, what soft lips! like Attic honey. But might she not stay with me?

EURIPIDES: Impossible, officer; good evening.

SCYTHIAN: Oh! oh! old woman, do me this pleasure.

EURIPIDES: Will you give a drachma?

SCYTHIAN: Aye, that I will.

EURIPIDES: Hand over the money.

SCYTHIAN: I have not got it, but take my quiver in pledge. I'll bring her back. [To the dancing girl] Follow me, my fine young wench. Old woman, you keep an eye on this man. But what's your name?

EURIPIDES: Artemisia.

SCYTHIAN: I'll remember it, Artemuxia. [He takes the dancing girl away.]

EURIPIDES: [aside] Hermes, god of cunning, receive my thanks! everything is turning out for the best. [To the flute-girl] As for you, friend, go along with them. Now let me loose his bonds. [To MNESILOCHUS] And you, directly I have released you, take to your legs and run off full tilt to your home to find your wife and children.

MNESILOCHUS: I shall not fail in that as soon as I am free.

EURIPIDES: [releasing MNESILOCHUS] There! It's done. Come, fly, before the Scythian lays his hand on you again.

MNESILOCHUS: That's just what I am doing. [Both depart in haste.]

SCYTHIAN: [returning] Ah! old woman! what a charming little girl! Not at all a prude, and so obliging! Eh! where is the old woman? Ah! I am undone! And the old man, where is he? Hi, old woman, old woman Ah! Ah! but this is a dirty trick! Artemuxia! she has tricked me, that's what the little old woman has done! Get clean out of my sight, you cursed quiver! [Picks it up and throws it across the stage.] Ha! you are well named quiver, for you have made me quiver indeed. Oh! what's to be done? Where is the old woman then? Artemuxia!

LEADER OF THE CHORUS: Are you asking for the old woman who carried the lyre?

SCYTHIAN: Yes, yes; have you seen her?

LEADER OF THE CHORUS: She has gone that way along with the old man.

SCYTHIAN: Dressed in a long robe?

LEADER OF THE CHORUS: Yes; run quick, and you will overtake them.

SCYTHIAN: Ah! rascally old woman! Which way has she fled? Artemuxia!

LEADER OF THE CHORUS: Straight on; follow your nose. But, hi! where are you running to now? Come back, you are going exactly the wrong way.

SCYTHIAN: Ye gods! ye gods! and all this while Artemuxia is escaping. [He runs off.]

LEADER OF THE CHORUS: Go your way! and a pleasant journey to you! But our sports have lasted long enough; it is time for each of us to be off home; and may the two goddesses reward us for our labours!

THE END

www.ReadHowYouWant.com

You can buy our **Large Type** and **EasyRead** books from our www.ReadHowYouWant.com website, from websites like Amazon.com and through your UK and North American bookshop.

EasyRead books are designed to make your reading easy and enjoyable. **EasyRead** books are published in different font sizes, so you can select the font size best for you.

EasyRead is for people with normal eyesight who want books in an easy-to-read format.

EasyRead Comfort is for people who find reading small print tiring but do not need large print.

EasyRead Large is for people who find it easier to read larger print.

The **EasyRead** font, character, word and line spacing have all been set to make it as easy as possible both to recognize a word, and to run your eye along a line of text without losing your place. We split as few words as possible at line ends, as split words make reading harder and can be annoying. For out-of-copyright books, words have been changed to modern spelling (where the sense is not affected), and the original hyphenation of compound words has been retained where this improves word recognition or sense.

With most things you buy, you get a choice, and you can choose the make and model that suits best. There is a big exception – books. You don't get to choose a format that is easy for you to read – you have to read the format the publisher selects.

This "**One Size Fits All**" paradigm **no longer** need apply to books.

At www.ReadHowYouWant.com, you can order a book just as you want it, so you can read it easily. You can choose nearly any format, and at a surprisingly low cost, because of a technical breakthrough that allows us to typeset an individual book automatically, print and bind the book and have it quickly sent directly to you.

You can have your book in **Talking Book** formats (**DAISY or MP3**) or as an **E-book** or in **Braille**.

We have developed totally new visual formats which we hope will help people with **dyslexia** and other print reading disabilities. Look at www.ReadHowYouWant.com for more information.

Good news for publishers and authors. There is a big market for large type, personalized and accessible format books. We can help publishers and authors find new market opportunities for their books, and selling your book through www.ReadHowY ouWant.com is easy – we do the work for you. Contact us on info@ReadHowYouWant .com.

Printed in Great Britain
by Amazon.co.uk, Ltd.,
Marston Gate.